CAVEBOY ♥ CRUSH

Words by
Beth Ferry

Pictures by
Joseph Kuefler

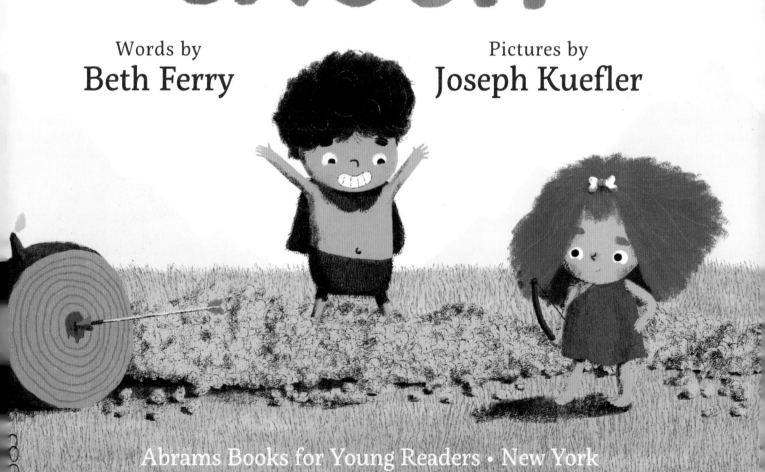

Abrams Books for Young Readers • New York

Neander was a typical caveboy.

He loved drawing on walls.

He loved chasing mammoth butterflies.

He loved his pet rock, Rock.

He also loved catching fish, which was exactly
what he was doing when he caught . . .

. . . a glimpse of the most beautiful girl in the prehistoric world.

She was short.
She was hairy.
She was perfect.

When she noticed him, Neander turned six shades of sunset and jumped into the lake.

When he finally surfaced,

she was gone.

Neander meandered home.
Everything he saw reminded him of the girl.

He mooned.

He moaned.

He grinned.

He groaned.

"Neander cranky?" Papa asked.
"No," said Mama.
"Neander crabby?"
"No," said Mama.
"Neander cross?"

"No," said Mama. "You remember."
"Oh," said Papa. "Crush."
Crush? thought Neander.
CRUSH!

Neander dashed to the Field of Bees.
He picked and plucked and plucked and picked.

Then he went to find the girl.

When he saw her, he grunted, "Me Neander."
She peered down and smiled.
"Me Neanne."
He dropped the flowers and said . . .

Crazy, thought Neanne.
Then she ran.

Neander was disappointed, but not for long.
Something grander, thought Neander.

Neander trekked to the Waves of Salt.

He swam and swum and swum and swam
until he spotted an enormous conch shell.

He carried the shell to her house

and blew into it with all
his might.

Then he said . . .

Cuckoo, thought Neanne.
Then she ran.

Neander was dismayed,
but not for long.

Mega extra super grander,
thought Neander.

He set off through the Field of Bees,

past the Waves of Salt,

until he arrived at the
Island of Icy Ice.

He picked the smallest enormous iceberg.
He lugged and tugged and tugged and lugged it back home.

"NEANNE!" he called. "Neanne! Neanne?"
But Neanne was . . . nowhere.

He could find neither hide nor hair of her.

Neander was crushed.

Drip.

Drop.

Droop.

But then he spied a sturdy shard of shell,
which sparked an idea.

Furiously he began

chipping,

chiseling,

carving,

creating.

It was a work of art straight from the heart.
Neanne stared at the sculpture.
She smiled, then said . . .

Cool, thought Neander.

And nothing could be grander.

For Chris, always
—B.F.

To everyone I crushed,
and to everyone who crushed me
—J.K.

Cataloging-in-Publication Data has been applied for and may be obtained
from the Library of Congress.

ISBN 978-1-4197-3656-8

Text copyright © 2019 Beth Ferry
Illustrations copyright © 2019 Joseph Kuefler
Book design by Pamela Notarantonio

Printed and bound in China
10 9 8 7 6 5 4 3 2

Abrams Books for Young Readers are available at special discounts when purchased in quantity for
premiums and promotions as well as fundraising or educational use. Special editions can also be
created to specification. For details, contact specialsales@abramsbooks.com or the address below.

Abrams® is a registered trademark of Harry N. Abrams, Inc.

ABRAMS The Art of Books
195 Broadway, New York, NY 10007
abramsbooks.com